PRAISE FOR ANGELA SLATTER

'Angela Slatter is a powerful and eloquent voice in horror fiction. Every story in this collection is a dark and polished gem.' ~ **Stephen Jones**, award winning editor

'Slatter's dark fantasies have a bright, burning core of understanding and insight.' ~ **M.R. Carey**, author of *The Girl with All the Gifts* and *The Boy on the Bridge*

'Angela Slatter is one of the treasures of current horror fiction. Her work is darkly magical, lyrical, and beautiful, and I can't recommend it highly enough.' ~ **Alison Littlewood**, author of *A Cold Season*, *The Unquiet House*, *A Cold Silence*, *The Path of Needles*

'Marvellous stuff! Angela Slatter confronts the darker side of humanity in these bracing meditations on the nature of belief, betrayal, and wonder. *Winter Children and Other Chilling Tales* is a riveting read, and a fine addition to the canon of one of the genre's fastest-rising stars.' ~ **Helen

Marshall, author of *Hair Side, Flesh Side* and *Gifts for the One Who Comes After*

'Angela Slatter's stories are enviably original, and told in prose as stylish as it's precise. Not just disturbing but often touching, her work enriches and revives the tale of terror.' ~ **Ramsey Campbell**, author of *The Doll Who Ate His Mother, The Hungry Moon,* and *Told by the Dead*

'Angela Slatter is an international treasure. She blends horror, fantasy, and fairy tale to create something entirely fresh, but which feels too like the nightmares half-forgotten when you were a child.' ~ **Robert Shearman**, author of *Love Songs for the Shy and Cynical, Remember Why You Fear Me,* and *They Do the Same Things Different There*

'Angela Slatter's wonderful collection is filled with tales of gruelling horror and shiver-inducing dread, often swathed in shades of the darkest humour. You won't want it to end.' ~ **Tim Lebbon**, author of *The Silence* and *The Hunt*

NO GOOD DEED

A SOURDOUGH TALE

ANGELA SLATTER

Brain Jar Press
PO Box 6687
Upper Mt Gravatt, QLD, 4122
Australia
www.BrainJarPress.com

Cover design by Peter Ball
Cover Image: Satika/Shutter-stock

ISBN: 978-1-922479-05-1

THANK YOU FOR BUYING THIS BRAIN JAR PRESS CHAPBOOK

ALSO BY KIRSTYN MCDERMOTT

Perfections

Madigan Mine

Caution: Contains Small Parts

Triquetra

ABOUT THE AUTHOR

Kirstyn McDermott has been working in the darker alleyways of speculative fiction for much of her career. She is the author of two award-winning novels, *Madigan Mine* and *Perfections*, and a collection of short fiction, *Caution: Contains Small Parts*. Her stories and poetry have been published in various magazines, journals and anthologies both within Australia and internationally, with her most recent work being *Never Afters*, a series of novellas that retell classic

Photo by Paul Ewins

fairy tales. She holds a PhD in creative writing with a research focus on re-visioned fairy tales and produces and co-hosts a literary discussion podcast, The Writer and the Critic. Kirstyn lives in Ballarat, Australia, with fellow writer Jason Nahrung and two distinctly non-literary felines. She can be found online at www.kirstynmcdermott.com.

NO GOOD DEED

Isobel hesitates outside the grand door to the chamber she'd thought to share with Adolphus. It's a work of art, with carven figures of Adam and Lilith standing in front of a tree, a cat at the base, a piece of fruit in transit between First Man and First Woman so one cannot tell if she offers to he, or otherwise.

Her recent exertions have drained what little strength she had, and the food she'd found in the main kitchen (all servants asleep, the odour of stale mead rising from them like swamp gas) sits heavily in a stomach shrunk so very small by a denial not hers. The polished wooden floorboards of the gallery are cold beneath her thin feet — so thin! Never so slender all her life. A little starvation will do wonders, she thinks. As she moved through the house, she'd caught sight of herself in more than one filigreed mirror and seen all the changes etched upon her: silver traceries in the dishevelled dark hair, face terribly narrow — who'd have known those fine cheekbones had lain beneath all that fat? — mouth still a cupid's bow pout and nose pert, but the eyes are sunken deep and, she'd almost swear to it, their colour changed from light green to deepest black as if night resides in them. The dress balloons around her new form, so much wasted fabric one might make a ship's sail from the excess.

How long before the plumpness returns? Before her cheeks have apples, the lines in her face are smoothed out? She can smell again, now, but all she can discern is the scent of her own body, unwashed for so long. A bath, she thinks longingly, then draws her attention back to where it needs to be: the door.

Or, rather, what lies behind it.

She reaches out, looks at the twiggish fingers, the black half-moons of dirt beneath the nails, how weirdly white her hand appears on the doorknob shaped like a wolf's head, so bulbous she can barely grasp it properly. She takes a deep, deep breath, and turns the handle.

Isobel woke with a weight on her eyes, cold and dead.

Her mouth, too, was similarly burdened: lips pressed down and thin metallic tendrils crept between them. Her forehead was banded by something chill and hard, a line running the length of her nose, her cheeks and chin encased; as if she wore a helmet she had no memory of applying before bed. She had no memory either of going to sleep. Her throat and arms were mercifully free, but chest, abdomen and hands were encumbered. Not a cage, then.

Remain calm, she told herself, *slow your breathing*. She'd been taught at St Dymphna's to assess situations carefully; easier said than done when you couldn't open your eyes.

Rings, she thought. *Rings on my fingers and bells on my toes.* She tried to wiggle her feet, found them unwilling to respond, still quite numb; pins and needles were beginning, however, so some sign of hope. Wrists encircled, entrapped by ... bracelets and bangles. She twitched her digits; only one finger bore a reasonable burden, a thin metal ribbon. Her husband's family, no matter their wealth, always insisted on a wedding band as plain as day. For love, they believed, must be unadorned.

My husband, she thought, and wondered where he was.

Adolphus Wollstonecraft.

Surely he'd not have deserted her? Not so soon at any rate. Then she recalled they'd only just been married. That this morning she was preparing for her marriage, surrounded by Adolphus' girl cousins, so numerous that she'd had to pause before addressing each one so as not to get a name wrong and thereby cause offense (excepting Cousins Enyd and Delwyn, of course, they'd become so close!). All of them dressed as bridesmaids for she had neither sisters, nor cousins, nor aunts, nor friends who might stand her this service; all of them a whirl of pastel colours and soft fabrics, the light from the candelabrums picking out the rich necklaces and earrings, brooches and hair ornaments, finer than any queen might own. Yet none as lovely as those Isobel brought with her, inheritances from mother and grandmothers, aunts and great-aunts, the items that came to Isobel because she was the last of her line, the single point where all things might end or begin again depending on the whims of her womb.

She ran her tongue over her teeth, prodded at the wires and was able to dislodge them with a dull, wet clink against the bone of her teeth. But there was something else: her canines were larger, augmented, and polished, a series of cool smoothnesses and sharp edges. She caught the tip of her tongue on one of those edges and tasted a burst of iron tang, imagined the bleed as a red blossoming.

She opened her mouth wider, felt the weight on her lips half-fall into the cavity; she turned her head, spat, and the mouthpiece fell away; the wires, reluctantly giving up their grip on her dentition, hit the softness she was lying on with a slithering *plink*. Whatever had been attached to her canines remained, however, so firmly affixed she was wary of interfering with them after that first cut. They would wait.

The weights over her eyes and face had also loosened with the movement of her head. She shook harder and with a tinkle and a chink they were gone, landing wherever the other things had. Whatever she reclined upon was soft but compacted by the weight of her body. How long had she been there?

Where was she?

Isobel opened her lids, though the lashes felt glued with sleep, with the sandman's dust. She blinked vigorously, but there was only blackness even when she widened her eyes. She closed them again, breathed slowly to calm herself, then shallowly when she realised the air was stale with a hint of old decay.

I am asleep, she thought. *I am asleep and dreaming in my marital bed.* But she still could not summon the details of her wedding eve, of neither feast nor fornication, and surely she should? Surely good or bad, she would remember that? The touches, the sighs, the delight? The pain, the weight, the imposition? Surely she'd recall at least one of the things the other girls at St Dymphna's had whispered of at night in their dormer attic when they should have been resting.

'I am asleep,' she said out loud. 'I am asleep and in my bridal bed.'

'Oh no, you're not,' came a voice from the darkness, brittle and raw, with a hint of amusement. Not Adolphus, no. A woman. A woman who'd not spoken in a very long time by the sound of it.

Isobel startled, jerked; things that weighed on her chest slipped and slid off with a jingle. She sat up, but her head connected with a rough low rock shelf; the skin parted at her hairline and she felt a slow welling of blood on her forehead. It took a while before she could speak.

'Who are you? Where am I?' The Misses Meyrick had always instructed their pupils to ask questions whenever they could: *You never know what skerrick of information might help you survive.*

'I am you,' answered the woman, and Isobel wondered if she'd gone mad, prayed to wake from the dream. 'Well, you *before* you, I suppose. And you are me, after me.'

'Don't speak in riddles! Tell me how to wake! I bid you, spirit, release me from this delusion!'

'Oh, you think yourself ridden by the mare of night?' The pitch lightened with surprise, then fragmented into giggles, each as sharp as a pin. There was an echo, too, wherever they were. Then the tone steadied, though mirth remained in evidence. 'Oh, no. Oh no, poor Isobel. You are sadly awake. Alert at long last.'

'Who are you? Why am I here? Where is my husband? I was at my wedding banquet ...' she trailed off, not truly able to remember if there was any trace of the feast in her mind. She thought she remembered someone – Adolphus' mother? – tugging the veil down over her face, readying her for the procession through the castle. Or was it Cousin Enyd? Or Cousin Delwyn? Or? Or? Or?

Someone had lifted the veil, certainly, for it bunched behind her head, pillowing her neck. Surely later, after *Volo* had been said, the echoes of the vows running along the walls and floor and vaulted ceiling of the small chapel, barely big enough to hold that fine family. So small a chapel, in fact, that only relatives had been bid to attend at the Wollstonecrafts' isolated estate.

And the Misses Meyrick. She cannot forget *them.*

Isobel's erstwhile school marms, not invited, had come anyway to watch, to witness the choice she'd made, all their good training, her mother's good money, gone to waste. They did not speak to her, neither Orla nor Fidelma, not a word of congratulation nor censure. Naught but disappointed looks as she and Adolphus walked down the aisle as man and wife.

There!

A memory, solid and stable. Pacing beside her handsome new husband, and the Misses Meyrick so far from their school for poison girls and looking at her as if she'd left their house to burn; left them to shame. So, not a happy memory but a memory nonetheless. A real one. A true one. Something to hold on to.

And another memory: the Misses Meyrick once again, at the wedding feast, waiting by the doors while the happy couple were greeted and congratulated by their guests. Isobel thinking *I must speak to them for they loved me in their own fashion!* So she'd picked her way through the crowd until she stood before her old instructors. Long moments passed before Fidelma spoke.

'Your mother,' she said, 'would be ashamed.'

Orla stepped behind her and Isobel felt terror like she never had before; but the woman merely said, 'Pish!' and showed her a hairpin with a long silver shaft and a jewelled head shaped like a daisy; the outer petals were of diamonds, and the floret, divided distinctly into two halves, of yellow topazes. Then she slid it into Isobel's finely constructed hairstyle, beneath the long veil so no one might see the ornament and note how exquisite it was. 'This,' said Orla, 'is the last thing we can do for you.'

Before she could reply, the Misses Meyrick seemed to fade from the room, although she knows she saw them move, saw them walk away with elegant contempt, yet somehow it seemed that it was not a mere exit they committed, but a Departure.

Then the other voice repeated, 'Wedding feast?' and Isobel was brought back to the stygian confines of ... wherever she was.

'Wedding feast, I remember my own. All those fine families, all those relations of blood, all of Adolphus' cousins and aunts and uncles. I had no one, myself, being an orphan of very rich parentage, but he said to me, "Kitten" – Kitty, actually, for he called me by that endearment – "Kitty, my sweet, they all adore you! It's like you're one of our very own, a true Wollstonecraft. Cousins Enyd and Delwyn say the same." And those very cousins sat beside me at the wedding feast, making sure I drank from my goblet the wine my husband poured for me and they considerately topped up.' The woman in the darkness cackled. 'Does this sound familiar?'

'Where am I?' asks Isobel in a very small voice. She did not say that it all sounded very familiar indeed. She carefully raised her hands until the fingertips touched the rough stone of the low ceiling. She inched them along, felt the scrape of rock, found a place where roof joined wall; but there was only the hint of a line, a thin parsimonious suggestion on her skin, not a chink, not a gap where air or light might creep in.

How many feet between where she lay and the ceiling? Three? Four? Ceiling? *Lid?* That last thought made her shudder and she shook it away.

'You're where you've been these past twelve months, sleeping like the dead.' The voice dropped low, secretive. 'But I knew you yet lived. I could hear the slow, slow beat of your heart, the slug-slug of your blood, the base breath that made your chest only just rise and fall.'

'Twelve months? Don't be a fool. I'd have died!'

'And you were meant to! But when you're so very nearly dead, everything becomes *unhurried*, blood, breath, appetite. You'll be ravenous soon, now that I've mentioned it.'

As if in response Isobel's stomach growled and cramped. She put a hand to it, discovered a kind of armour there, a lumpen embossed corset that might well turn aside a knife blade. At its sides she located small latches, which opened easily; presumably no one expected the dead to undress themselves.

'The poison they used,' mused her companion, 'is a strange mix: too little and it will render you ill, too much it will send you into a sleep undiscernible from true death, but if the amount is *juuust* right, then and only then you'll die. And it was new when used on me, so I died. It was old when used on you and Adolphus panicked and used too much, so you but slept.'

'You're lying. You're mad.'

'Oh, ho! Mad am I? That's possible, I suppose, I've been here a long while with only my thoughts, waiting for you to wake, and before that no one but myself to talk to. Who wouldn't go a little mad?' A sigh shifted the blackness, Isobel was almost certain she could see it. 'Shall I show you? Where we are? Then we can discuss my mendacity or otherwise. Well?'

'Yes,' said Isobel faintly.

For a second there was nothing, no sound, no movement, and then: a light. A tiny pinprick of luminous green, a point that pulsed and grew, strengthened and increased its ambit. The glow lit upon the things that had fallen from Isobel when she sat so precipitously; it caught at their lovely edges, lodged in facets, made it appear as if a hundred small fires had kindled on the musty purple silk.

She was distracted by a king's ransom in jewellery, but not of a common sort. Rich and rare, the cut and settings were of ancient design, almost foreign it was so antique, and Isobel could not think of where she'd seen its like before. None of it was hers, not one piece of the Lawrence family jewels to be seen, not a *single* thing she recognised. She put a hand to the back of her head, beneath the veil which had become odd in its texture, and found the one gem no one knew she had — no one but the Meyricks — the hairpin, its cool hard daisy arrangement reassuring.

Then she gazed around the space, found it to be a box, six feet by six feet by four, a flattened mattress beneath her. Such a small room! A bed-closet perhaps, but no sign of a door, of any egress. And that mattress ... not like any she'd ever seen, without either ticking or calico, neither down nor rushes to make it plump, but there was the smell of old lavender ... no, more like ... the lining for a death bed.

She sought her companion. Saw ...

Saw ...

Saw nothing but a skeleton in a jaundiced wedding dress, blue and gold boots with silver buttons up the side, a manically grinning skull from which red hair and a lopsided veil hung. The body was adorned with strange bijoux akin to those Isobel herself had worn.

And the body was glowing; glowing with the same green luminescence that had shown Isobel her location.

Isobel remembered at last that she'd seen such exquisite corpses before, in places where the wealthy venerated their dead and turned them into glittering saints. Old families and High Church. The Wollstonecrafts carried both in their bloodline.

And Isobel, comprehending at last where she was, began to scream.

The room, the Master's Chamber, is redolent of stale alcohol, spent seed and strong tobacco or perhaps incense. Some kind of drug? Isobel notices a kind of pipe in one corner, perhaps three feet high, made of blown glass in colours that have the same sheen as oil on water. There are silken tassels and a mouth piece and tubing. She'd heard of such things at St Dymphna's: Hepsibah Ballantyne had averred it a fine way to poison someone. Mistress Ballantyne had always said that to best murder another, one should discover their habits and run parallel to them, insert your lethal blow into the usual flow of their life, so that way the difference you made would most like not be noticed.

Isobel looks to the bed which is located beneath a bank of diamond-paned glass. In said bed, so enormous that it might fit six, she sees three figures. The covers are thrown back, as are the window shutters, for the eve is balmy, moonlit; one of her nannies always said that sleeping in moonlight let madness in. How many Wollstonecrafts have slept thus?

Spring, just, she thinks, *it was winter when I married*. A summer bride, lying winter-cold for so very long. No mourning for Adolphus, she notes, and no sleeping alone.

Her husband lies between the recumbent figures of Cousins Enyd and Delwyn, their dark Wollstonecraft locks spread tousled across crisp white pillowcases, their naked forms on crumpled sheets. Two girls Isobel had thought friends or like to become so. Their slumber is that of the well-used. There can be no mistaking it; the dead bride did not lie. She did not need to when she'd said *The*

Wollstonecrafts breed only amongst themselves and they are prolific, hiding those whose their parents are too closely related in attics and cellars, hiding those who show too much the double, triple, quadruple blossoming of blood.

Isobel thinks, memories flooding now, of all those Wollstonecrafts at the wedding feast, watching her so avidly. She wonders how she ever thought their eyes gleamed with love and happiness, their lips curved in welcome, not avarice. Perhaps she could not see their greed because her own was so intense as she gulped from the bridal cup held by Adolphus, offered so generously to her first — against tradition! — a sign of his devotion, his love for his young wife. She has, even now, no recollection of falling asleep at the table, of drifting into what her new family thought was death. There is only the memory of the cup, the dark liquid within, her husband's tender smile.

Nor does she even now recollect crossing the wide room, yet somehow she is standing beside the great bed, staring down at Cousin Enyd whose tiny waist she's always admired; on Enyd's left wrist is a diamond bracelet that had belonged to Isobel's mother. Isobel's hand goes to the back of her own head, fidgets beneath the friable veil and finds the hair pin that was the final gift of Orla and Fidelma Meyrick. The gems and metal are cool against her fingers and the pin comes out with no complaint. Isobel looks at it carefully, remembers the instructions from one of the weaponry classes, then gives a nod of satisfaction. These three have been drinking, smoking, heavily; all of them snore. They'll not wake easily.

She leans over Cousin Enyd, lowers the hairpin point-first to the cockleshell of the ear facing her, then depresses the left side of the daisy's centre. A single tiny drop of paralytic poison, so powerful she fears to get it on her own skin, oozes from the tip of the pin and drips into shadowy coil of Enyd's ear. Isobel waits for a count of five, then swiftly plunges the shaft into the narrow canal; her fingers push the right side of the daisy design and the length of the pin splits into four very fine, very sharp, very tough lengths which tear into the brain. Cousin Enyd hardly moves, giving just the tiniest of shudders as she voids her bladder and bowels, but the stink of it barely registers above the other rich scents in the room.

Isobel creeps softly around the other side of the bed and repeats the process on Cousin Delwyn, whose rich thick curls she'd often envied; around this one's swan-like neck is the emerald and pearl locket that had belonged to Isobel's grandmother. Delwyn dies no more noisily than did Enyd, though she is fleshier, larger, there is less poison and the paralysis is not so entire; she twitches, kicks too close to Adolphus and Isobel must swiftly grab at the limb, hold it in place until the tremors still. Isobel feels a twinge of pride; the time at St Dymphna's was neither wasted nor its lessons lost. Orla Meyrick herself couldn't have executed these deaths anymore tidily.

Adolphus still has not stirred.

Isobel slips her stolen jewellery into the hidden pocket of her dress, then steps away, takes up position between the bed and the door. Her breathing remains steady — it did not change even as she slaughtered those false cousins — and what she feels moving through her is a cold thing, a passionless fury, a determination to one end. She takes a breath and begins to sing.

'ARE YOU QUITE FINISHED?' came the voice when Isobel at last ran out of breath and fear. 'Pride of St Dymphna's you are.'

'How do you know——'

'I've had twelve months to wander around in your sleeping mind — no point looking like that. I'm bored and have been for a very long time. A saint couldn't have stopped herself. I can't do anything else, can't move from here; I've only got a little energy and I'm saving that for something rather more special than a mere haunting.'

'How did I get here? How did *you* get here?!' wept Isobel, stung by the corpse's callousness.

'Our husband, you little fool! Adolphus Wollstonecraft. We're not the first brides he's disposed of for the sake of their fortunes, but *you* were the first one who was supposed to kill him. And failed to do so quite spectacularly. Imagine all the trouble you could have saved. No doubt, there'll be more betrotheds after us when his goodly period of mourning is done, and all your wealth run through!'

'How many?' asked Isobel, shocked out of her sobs.

'Four. Buried on the other side of the altar. I'm sure they've got fresh new maidens picked out to take up residence beside us in the fullness of time.'

'But you can talk, make this light …'

'And small, bitter consolation that it is. As I said, I can't haunt anyone. Hepsibah Ballantyne knows her business too well for that.'

Isobel startles at the name, thinks about the poisons mistress who came to St Dymphna's and taught the girls to brew dark potions. There were whispers that the woman was a coffin-maker, too, and indeed that was where her renown lay; the facility with poison was a happy coincidence and a secret for St Dymphna's headmistresses and students. A lucrative habit borne of her more-than-passing interest in death.

'My, what interesting things you keep hidden in your heart and head. I only knew her name from conversations I'd heard Adolphus and his mother have as they crossed the floor above my tomb — they've a fondness for plotting in the chapel, perhaps it makes them feel justified and holy.' The corpse sounded sad.

'Poison,' says Isobel.

'And there are these jewels, of course. Not contented with paying a premium for death-beds to keep us beneath, they laid these cursed gems over us.'

Isobel prodded at the attachments to her canines, and the dead bride said, 'Those are to stop us from becoming vampires or some other such blood ghosts. They made us saints against our will, the ecstatic dead to cover their crimes, to keep us from haunting them, from ever getting vengeance.'

'But I'm not dead,' said Isobel softly.

'No, indeed you are not!' Gleeful now. 'None of the chains the living have placed upon you have taken, sweet Isobel, and you are fit for my purpose!'

Isobel listened, watched the still form; there was only the sickly pulsing green light to tell her she wasn't truly alone, that the voice wasn't simply in her head. But what if it *was*? What if the light was an hallucination too? Perhaps this was her punishment.

Punishment for what?

For leaving St Dymphna's the moment her mother died?

For denying her duty?

For falling in love with the man she was meant to murder?

For being so foolish as to trust?

'Why did you do it? Trust him? You were better off than any of us. You were trained. You had goal, a duty.'

'Get out of my head! I'm conscious now and I don't appreciate you using it as your playground!' Isobel shouted so loudly that her ears hurt in the confined space.

'I'm sorry,' said the dead bride. 'There's little call for etiquette down here so I forget.'

'For him. He was older by a little, funny, sweet and smart. He didn't care that I was fat. He was … kind. I met him before I was sent to St Dymphna's. I knew almost from the cradle what I was meant to do, that the very point of my life was to destroy another's — to avenge an ancient and dusty death, an ancestress of mine murdered at the hands of his forefathers.' Isobel paused. 'But I met him and I loved him from the first even though I knew I shouldn't. I thought … I thought I might draw it out, put off taking his life until after my mother died, until there was no one left to care. Then he and I could be happy, the past forgotten, dead and buried.

'Then my mother did die, sooner rather than later, before I'd even finished my schooling. I left St Dymphna's the very day after the news arrived. I went to him, went to his home, we planned our life together.'

'They're not as fabulously prosperous as they appear, you know. There's much tat and shine for show, but the vaults are empty, more often than not with but a few pieces of gold, candlesticks and crested salvers. The family silver has been pawned and redeemed time and again − the silversmiths of Caulder know the Wollstonecrafts of old.'

'But—'

'Rich brides are this family's business. We're lambs to them, meat on the table, money in the bank, brides in caskets. Did you not wonder that there were no friends invited to your nuptials? None there but Wollstonecrafts? That they live so far from anything despite their supposed wealth? It's hard to keep secrets in cities where everyone's watching to see what you do, where the well-to-do keep better track of their daughters.' A long sigh. 'You signed over everything, didn't you? All the riches your mother gathered, the businesses she built, all the prosperity and majesty that clever merchant queen reaped from her investments over the years, and you signed it away for a piece of cock.' A giggle, rueful. 'Don't feel too great a fool, I did the same, and brides before me and thee who were otherwise reckoned clever. I … I was ugly, yet he convinced me he loved me, that he cared not a jot for beauty.'

'But Adolphus *loved* me. He didn't know what I gave up for him, that I put his life first.' But she thought of the tiny moments, the signs she'd ignored: all the occasions when plans for what came after the wedding were put off, discussions avoided. *Don't you worry about that, my dear, we've plenty of time for that later.* Yet how quickly he'd begged she sign documents that transferred her ownerships to him in case of a dreadful tragedy, which would of course never happen.

'You think not? The poison he used came from Ballantyne, who knew you at the school, who outfitted this very coffin-tomb, this death-bed just as she did the others — she's not so skilled with stone as wood but she did a good enough job to trap me. You let him live, Isobel, but no good deed ever goes unpunished.' The skeleton gave a rueful chuckle. 'And I doubt you're the first poison girl to flee that venerable institution, to choose love over duty.'

'I was, you know. The Misses told me with great relish and umbrage,' confessed Isobel.

'Ah. My tale is your tale, or at least so close that the differing details barely matter. But at last something can be done.' The voice rose like a victory hymn.

'You're dead,' said Isobel, toneless, lifeless. 'You're dead and I'm trapped. Even if he's betrayed me,' — *if?* — 'nothing can be done.'

'Do you have the engagement ring he gave you? An

enormous sapphire, if memory serves correct, blue as a hot afternoon sky?'

Isobel examined her fingers, looked to where the item in question should be, but there were only the ornate rings joined to each other by golden chains, the things meant to hold her in place. She pulled them off, added them to the glittering pile beside her.

'No. Just the wedding band,' mused the dead bride. 'The same for all of us. No point in wasting an engagement ring when you can reuse it, like a dog collar. They don't want to trouble themselves with a costly replacement, and they can't use *these*,' — Isobel knew she meant the cursed things — 'Gods forbid anything should happen to the *lamb* before the wedding, before the Wollstonecrafts get the fortune for which they've worked so hard!'

Isobel looked at the other's skeletal hands, wrapped around a posy of dead yet somehow intact roses. A strong breeze would interrupt their carefully held structure. On one finger she could make out the dull gleam of a ring identical to hers.

'I'll die here,' she said. 'I'll starve as a trusting fool deserves to. I'll suffocate.' Suddenly the air felt thinner, staler, her lungs more demanding. 'But I'll go mad first.'

'And what a delightful change that will be,' sniggered the dead bride.

'You'll not likely starve any time soon, although you're looking thin, yet not so thin as I. There's plenty of air, you silly bint. As for madness, sometimes by taking refuge in it for a time is the only way to maintain a modicum of sanity.'

Isobel realised then that her own dress — with all the ribbons and frills and bows meant to make her beautiful, but just made her look even more enormous — was terribly, terribly large on her. That none of the weight she'd carried around all her life, that drove her mother and nannies to despair, remained. Reading her thoughts again, the dead one said, 'Bet you never expected you'd be grateful for that fat! What do you think kept you alive all these months?'

'I don't want to live,' wailed Isobel, knowing it was stupid as soon as the words were out.

'Ye gods, the stock at St Dymphna's is poor. A man betrayed you and you want to die?'

'No. I ... I betrayed my mother, my teachers, by trusting him, by choosing him.' Isobel thought of the Misses Meyrick and their steely countenances.

'And you think dying is the choice they'd want you to select? You, upon whom so much effort was expended to make you more *active*?' The dead bride tut-tutted. 'It would be easier, certainly, to expire, but St Dymphna's girls, as I understand it, aren't made for easy paths. You weren't descended from milksops or weeping maidens; the women before you carried sword and shield, they fought in the open, their blood was red and rich and violent! It's in your veins, Isobel, so pull yourself together!'

'But I can't get out—'

'Of course you can, there's a way, a way for the living.'

Isobel sat up at straight as she could, stared at the unmoving form. 'How?'

'Ah, now that's information for which you must bargain, Isobel girl.'

'Tell me now or I swear I'll scatter your bones, I'll grind them to dust even if it makes my fingers bleed!'

'That's the spirit! Now calm down. In return for my very useful knowledge, you will make me a promise, a promise by which you'll set more store than ever before or so help me—'

Isobel did not pause. 'I will promise you anything, just get me out of this tomb!'

THE SONG IS one the dead bride advised, tried to teach until Isobel comprehended that she already knew from her old life, a tune sung by this nanny or that governess. Her husband does not stir, so she sings louder still for there's no one to wake but Adolphus. She wonders how he's spent his days since her death, then decides she can probably guess. Sings more loudly, more sweetly, until her patience runs out and she fair shouts, 'Adolphus!'

He sits up, stunned, blinking in that strange mix of darkness and moonlight and receding sleep that renders him blind for long moments. He does not notice the still bodies of his cousins on either side of him, does not spare them a glance. He sees only Isobel.

She imagines she must look close to the spectre he tried so hard to make her. She smiles and follows the script. 'Adolphus, my love, fear not. You're simply dreaming.'

She can see him struggling to recognise her and she remembers how changed she is from the lumbering lumpy girl he said he loved above all others. That all those places he caressed and fondled and fingered are so much easier to find now.

'It's Isobel, my love. See you dream me how I truly was, how I truly wished to be. Still you know my heart!'

'But you're dead, my Isobel.' Fear silvers his tone.

'Oh yes! So very dead and you do but dream me, but there is something I must tell you, something that threatens your very house and future. My love has drawn me back. Will you follow me and see?'

'But of course! That you should still care for me beyond death! It warms my heart,' he says and creeps to the end of the bed so as not to disturb his cousins' rest. He reaches for her and Isobel holds up a warning hand.

'The living cannot touch the dead, my love! Lest you be drawn down to lie beside me.' Adolphus nods. Isobel smiles. 'Then follow and allow me to render you this last service.'

The moment she turns her back she knows it for a mistake, but she was brimming with confidence that her deception had worked, that she'd *won*. She can almost feel Orla and Fidelma's disapproving stares just as she can feel the steel of her husband's fingers closing around her left wrist.

'Little fool, little bitch! Do you think I've not created enough ghosts to know one? That I cannot tell the smell of warm blood from cold? "My love has drawn me back." Gods, what a lackwit you must think me, as much of a one as yourself.'

Isobel struggles, but her strength is so depleted from her long slumber that she cannot make any headway.

'Fear not, sweet Isobel, I'll put you back where you belong.'

Isobel kicks him in the groin, watches with not inconsiderable delight as he doubles over, then she remembers to flee. She flings the door closed behind her, starts towards the grand staircase. She is halfway down when she hears the crash of wood against wall that says her husband is in pursuit. Her strength is fading, her speed bleeding to nothing. At the bottom of the stairs she must cross the marble floor, pass through the darkened arched doorway, and down the few worn steps into the chapel, and thence to the altar.

What if he catches her first?

What if he takes it in his head to strangle her then and there for there's no one who might look for her, no one to suspect she lives, there are no appearances to be maintained. Even if some family member of his might wander by, they've no cause to save her. From behind comes a growl, a roar of such surpassing anger and viciousness that she finds her feet have wings. An extra burst of speed gets her to the entrance hall, almost skidding on marble tiles as she goes. When she passes through the doorway she does not touch the steps, but rather flies several yards into the chapel, landing at the third row of pews, the impact jarring every bone in her body, so much so that she's sure she must rattle. She stumbles her way towards the altar with its shimmer of precious plate, and splashes of colour on the bright white cloth covering where moonlight pierces the stained glass window.

Adolphus is enraged, he'll not see the open tombs, the floor slid back by dint of the hidden switches the dead bride told her about, a handy bit of knowledge plucked from one of the passing ghosts of the Wollstonecrafts' castle, a stonemason who'd built the secret passages and the tombs at the request of a great-great-great Wollstonecraft grandfather whose terror was to be buried alive. But such escapes are no use to the dead, and the grandparent was indeed thoroughly deceased when put into the sepulchre — although his bones and those of other departed were shifted and shuffled when the present generation began their business of burying brides. The stone mason himself, another trusting fool, had been put to death as soon as the work was completed.

This plan, fumes Isobel, was not best thought-out and she resents the dead bride for not having formulated a better strategy in all her time lying in the crypt. Then again, perhaps she never was very practical in life. Isobel, St Dymphna's drop-out though she might be, is quite certain she'd have come up with something — *anything* — better.

Adolphus does not see the four figures slumped in the front pews, and Isobel runs past them, skidding to a halt at the altar. Her husband comes to a stop a foot from her, cursing and spitting and telling her precisely what he thought of her in life and death; if she had any lingering doubts about his role in her demise they are dispelled once and for all.

'I will put you back in the ground, sweet Isobel. Although these months beneath have done you good, who'd have thought under all that fat you were so terribly lovely?'

'Would it have stopped you from murdering me?' she asks out of sheer curiosity.

He shakes his head, his grin is a wolf's. 'No. But I might have taken a little more fun with you. I might do so now. I have, after all, a husband's rights.'

'Will you exercise them on all of us?' Isobel says quietly, so calmly that he is thrown off by her lack of fear, her lack of panic.

'Us?' He tilts his head. 'Madness, I suppose, from the darkness.'

'Madness no doubt, but one you will share, my love. Come, greet your maidens, they wait at your back like good wives.'

Adolphus, seemingly unwilling to take his eyes from her, turns his head only a little, but it is enough for him to see what waits in the periphery. Four of his spouses, skeletons all, released them from their beds and gilded cages by Isobel, stand with effort, bones a'clacking and a'creaking, hair falling from heads to shoulders, and thence into empty rib cages. Their frocks have entirely decayed, leaving only threads and rags caught here in a joint, there on a bone, as if they might display to their husband their nakedness entire, in mimicry of the wedding night he denied them. There is, however, no sign of cartilage or tendons or muscles to show how they might be held together. Sheer will and malice, imagines Isobel, and not a little magic resulting from both.

She takes in the skulls with their hairline fractures, the stains decay has left, the wisps of hair that was once so glorious. At least one has a limp, another lacks an arm; a brigade of the halt and the lame, the obese and the damned ugly, all especially susceptible to any scrap of kindness, and unwary that their value to their husband was no greater than monetary. She wonders if the dead bride — her companion and guide — was a witch in life, undiscovered, for her powers to remain so long after death. Or perhaps she was simply a girl with hopes and dreams that curdled dark and sour and kept the strongest part of her, the bravest part, the worst part, alive.

Adolphus has gone astonishingly pale, as if his blood has turned coward and fled. His lips move, producing only, 'Whuh, whuh, whuh.'

'"Whuh?" What are you trying to say, my love? What is this sorcery? None but what you created yourself by murder and deceit.'

The brides shuffle forward, closing in on Adolphus who backs away, hands raised as if that will stop their awful progress with its accompanying symphony of clacking and rattling.

'What I want you to know, my love, is this: tonight your house will fall. I will put every Wollstonecraft here to the sword. Then I will make it my business to hunt down every bastard, bitch and by-blow who fell from your family tree and destroy them too. Your bloodline will be wiped from the face of the earth, and I swear before you and your wives that I shall make this my life's work.'

The corpse brides reach towards their husband, thin fingers, bony arms, ravaged joints, and with a cry Adolphus steps backwards. He does not see the open maw behind him, so he falls, arms windmilling, then there is a silence as he drops, then the *whump!* and *crack!* as he lands, dust flying into the air.

Isobel and the brides peer over the edge.

Adolphus lies in the tomb Isobel so recently occupied, recumbent upon the form of the dead bride, her own cursed jewellery removed. Isobel is sure she can see some broken bones on the skeletal girl where the impact has been too much, but while Adolphus remains stunned the dead bride's arms begin to move. They curve up and over, around her husband before he realises what's going on. The fingers of her right hand clench together into a spear and this she plunges into Adolphus' chest, the flesh of which parts as if it is no more than warm butter. There is the breaking of ribs prised apart and the wet sucking sound of red muscle meat being found and enclosed by a bony cage of palm and fingers.

'Your heart, my love,' says the dead bride, 'shall ever be mine.'

And with that there is a great sigh as from many mouths. Adolphus ceases to move, his eye glaze over. The girl in the tomb does not answer when Isobel calls, and she can no longer sense any presence other than her own. The chorus of brides falls to the flagstones, becomes dust even as Isobel watches. She is meticulous, though, ensuring they will have somewhere to rest, and brushes their final remains into the crypt. It falls on Adolphus and his penultimate bride like confetti for the dead. Isobel, feeling bereft that she cannot say goodbye to her sisters, whispers farewell and hopes they will hear it somewhere. She locates the switch to close the lid of the tomb, and then the second one that puts the floor back in place. When she is done it looks as if nothing ever happened here.

Isobel rises. There are weapons to be had in the house, sabres and stilettos that hang on walls for display, but will be just as fine used for their true purpose. She will spill all the blood to be found, she will put them to the sword and then set fire to the hangings in the bedrooms, the parlours, the grand hall. She will burn the place utterly to the ground.

No full graduate of St Dymphna's could do better, she is certain. She'll not return to the Misses Meyrick, though she might write to them from time to time as she crosses another Wollstonecraft off her list. Isobel will not hunt Hepsibah Ballantyne, for she was merely doing her job, and the poison used on Isobel was not *intended* for her. Oh, she'll find the coffin-maker, use her for her own ends — it's a fool who wastes a good poisons woman — but first of all she'll put a good scare into Hepsibah Ballantyne just for fun. She might even keep the gems on her canines long enough to give Ballantyne a glittering, terrifying smile.

Isobel takes one last look at the chapel, finds she cannot distinguish the joins where the floor might open up again if she were to press the right parts of the frieze carved into the altar. And she understands, then, the only thing that will truly haunt her as she goes upon her way: that she did not ask the dead bride, the one who came before her, for her name.

AUTHOR'S NOTE

"No Good Deed" first appeared in Mark Morris's *New Fears: Volume One* (and was reprinted in Stephen Jones' *Best New Horror #29* as "A Song of Dust"). I'd read *Heavenly Bodies: Cult Treasures & Spectacular Saints from the Catacombs* by Paul Koudounaris, and become fascinated (obsessed) by the idea of bejewelled saints in church crypts.

I'd used the idea before in a story set in the Sourdough universe, but I wanted to add something more to it: hence the idea of the bewitched death jewellery to help keep the dead beneath. (I've also used it again in "The Promise of Saints" in *The Tallow-Wife and Other* Tales.) I wanted to have an early St Dymphna's poison girl as my main character and to revisit the Misses Meyrick and Hepsibah Ballantine (from *The Bitterwood Bible and Other Recountings*).

And I also wanted to plant an ancestress for Cordelia and Bethany Lawrence who feature in the third Sourdough cycle mosaic, *The Tallow-Wife and Other Tales*. One day I'd like to write a novel about the Misses Meyrick and who they were before they started St Dymphna's School for Poison Girls.

THE FOLLOWING features all the *Sourdough* stories to date in chronological, rather than publication, order.

No Good Deed (Chapbook) 2021, Brain Jar Press

The Bitterwood Bible and Other Recountings
(Mosaic Collection) 2014, Tartarus Press

- "The Coffin-Maker's Daughter"
- "The Maiden In The Ice"
- "The Badger Bride"
- "The Burnt Moon"
- "By My Voice I Shall Be Known"
- "The Undone and the Divine"
- "The Night Stair"
- "Now, All Pirates are Gone"
- "St Dymphna's School for Poison Girls"
- "The Bitterwood Bible"
- "Terrible as an Army with Banners"

- "By The Weeping Gate"
- "Spells for Coming Forth By Daylight"

Sourdough and Other Stories (Mosaic Collection)
2010, Tartarus Press

- "The Shadow Tree"
- "Gallowberries"
- "Little Radish"
- "Dibblespin"
- "The Navigator"
- "The Angel Wood"
- "Ash"
- "The Story of Ink"
- "Lost Things"
- "A Good Husband"
- "A Porcelain Soul"
- "The Bones Remember Everything"
- "Sourdough"
- "Sister, Sister"
- "Lavender and Lychgates"
- "Under The Mountain"

Of Sorrow and Such (Novella) 2015, Tor.com

The Tallow-Wife (Novella) 2017, Fablecroft Press

The Tallow-Wife and Other Tales (Mosaic Collection)
2021, Tartarus Press

- "The Promise of Saints"
- "The Tallow-Wife"
- "What Shines Brightest Burns Most Fiercely"
- "Embers and Ash"

- "Bearskin"
- "The Nightingale and the Rose"
- "Of Ghosts and Glory"
- "A Stitch in Time"
- "Sleeping Like Snow"
- "Crossroads"
- "And A Young Husband to Bury Me"
- "By Such Paths"

All the Murmuring Bones (Novel) 2021, Titan Books

SOURDOUGH STORIES

Sourdough & Other Stories

The Bitterwood Bible & Other Recountings

The Tallow Wife & Other Stories

Of Sorrow & Such

All the Murmuring Bones as *A.G. Slatter* (Forthcoming)

COLLECTIONS

The Girl With No Hands & Other Tales

Midnight & Moonshine (with Lisa L. Hannett)

The Female Factory (with Lisa L. Hannett)

Black Winged Angels

Winter Children & Other Chilling Tales

A Feast Of Sorrows: Stories

The Heart Is a Mirror For Sinners & Other Stories

Red New Day & Other Micro-fictions

VERITY FASSBINDER

Vigil

Corpselight

Restoration

ABOUT THE AUTHOR

Angela Slatter is the author of the supernatural crime novels *Vigil*, *Corpselight* and *Restoration* from Jo Fletcher Books, as well as nine short story collections, including *The Girl with No Hands and Other Tales*, *Sourdough and Other Stories*, *The Bitterwood Bible and Other Recountings*, and *A Feast of Sorrows: Stories*. She is also the author of the novellas, *Of Sorrow and Such* and *Ripper*.

Vigil was nominated for the Dublin Literary Award in 2018, and Angela has won a World Fantasy Award, a British Fantasy Award, a Ditmar, an Australian Shadows Award and six Aurealis Awards. She has recently signed a two-book deal with Titan Books for *All The Murmuring Bones* and *Morwood*, gothic fantasies set in the world of the *Sourdough* and *Bitterwood* collections.

Angela's short stories have appeared in Australian, UK and US *Best Of* anthologies such *The Mammoth Book of New Horror, The Year's Best Dark Fantasy and Horror, The Best Horror of the Year, The Year's Best Australian Fantasy and Horror,* and *The Year's Best YA Speculative Fiction*. Her work has been translated into Bulgarian, Chinese, Russian, Italian, Spanish, Japanese, Polish, French and Romanian. Victoria Madden of Sweet Potato Films (*The Kettering Incident*) has optioned the film rights to one of her short stories ("Finnegan's Field").

She has an MA and a PhD in Creative Writing, is a graduate of Clarion South 2009 and the Tin House Summer Writers Workshop 2006, and in 2013 she was awarded one of the inaugural Queensland Writers Fellowships. In 2016 Angela was the Established Writer-in-Residence at the Katharine Susannah Prichard Writers Centre in Perth. She has been awarded career development funding by Arts Queensland, the Copyright Agency and, in 2017/18, an Australia Council for the Arts grant.

Find her online at www.angelaslatter.com

facebook.com/angelaslatterauthor

twitter.com/AngelaSlatter

instagram.com/angelaslatter

amazon.com/Angela-Slatter/e/B005QQ9FOA

THANK YOU FOR BUYING THIS
BRAIN JAR PRESS CHAPBOOK

To receive special offers, bonus content, and info on
new releases and other great reads, visit us
online at www.BrainJarPress.com

9 781922 479051